For Molly

First published in Great Britain in 2008 by
Piccadilly Press Ltd, 5 Castle Road, London NW1 8PR
www.piccadillypress.co.uk

Designed by Simon Davis
Printed and bound in China by WKT
Colour reproduction by Dot Gradations

ISBN: 978 1 85340 941 7 (hardback)
978 1 85340 940 0 (paperback)

1 3 5 7 9 10 8 6 4 2

Little Croc
and Bird

Tony Maddox

Piccadilly Press • London

Little Croc was always getting into trouble.

He just couldn't help it!

'Play nicely!' said Mummy Croc.
'Don't annoy the other animals!'
said Daddy Croc.

'OK,' sighed Little Croc . . . but he soon forgot!

He ran across the backs of the hippos.

He shouted at the zebras and made them jump.

He swung on the monkeys' tails . . .

and sent the parrots into a panic!

Little Croc was so naughty,
everyone hid when they
saw him coming.
'Oh good,' he said. 'No more silly
animals to get in my way!'

So Little Croc
played by himself –
and he always won!

He played throwing
games and he always
threw the furthest.

He played hide and seek and
no one ever found him.

'I've won again!' said Little Croc.
But suddenly it seemed very
quiet and Little Croc felt lonely.

As he lay wondering what to do next,
a small bird flew down and perched
on his back.

'I'll be your friend if you promise
to play nicely,' said Bird.

'That's the trouble,' sighed Little Croc.
'I want to be nice but I'm not very good at it!'

'It's quite easy,' said Bird,
'if you really try!'

'Hmm . . .' said Little Croc thoughtfully.
'Could you show me?'
'Of course!' said Bird.

So Bird showed Little Croc
how to chase butterflies without
hurting them . . .

how to swing on branches without
scaring the parrots . . .

and how to play hide
and seek together.

Then they lay on their backs and watched the
fluffy white clouds drifting across the sky.
'I like having a friend,' said Little Croc.

As the days passed, Little Croc made friends
with all the other animals too.

He pulled thorns from the leopard's paw with his strong jaws.

He untangled the
snakes when they
got themselves
in a muddle.

He combed the
knots out of
the lion's mane . . .

and he gave the meerkats rides across the river.

Mummy and Daddy Croc were
so proud of Little Croc.

And if Little Croc felt like doing something mischievous,
Bird was there to make sure he didn't.

At last, Little Croc
had learned how
to play nicely . . .

Well, **most** of the time!